Two Brown Bears

Martin
Waddell

Illustrated by
Steve Lavis

• • dingles & company

First published in the United States of America in 2008 by
dingles & company
P.O. Box 508
Sea Girt, New Jersey 08750

First Printing

Website: www.dingles.com
E-mail: info@dingles.com

Library of Congress Catalog Card Number
2007906323

ISBN
978-1-59646-956-3 (library binding)
978-1-59646-957-0 (paperback)

Two Brown Bears
Text © Martin Waddell, 2002
This U.S. edition of *Two Brown Bears*, originally published in English
in 2007, is published by arrangement with Oxford University Press.

The moral rights of the author have been asserted.
Database right Oxford University Press (maker).

Printed in China

Contents

Flying Bears

Chapter 1

The No-Wings Bear

One day, Harriet Bear was riding her bicycle. She saw Joe Bear.

Joe was bouncing up and down, up and down, flapping his arms. "I'm trying to fly," explained Joe. "Bears can't fly," Harriet said.

"Why can't bears fly?" asked Joe.

"They haven't got wings," said Harriet.

"But I *want* to fly in the sky," said Joe. He sounded very sad.

"I've got a Bear Plan," Harriet said. "I'll make us a Bear Pedal Plane!"

Harriet made a list of the things that they would need.

Things that Bears need for making Bear Pedal Planes by Harriet Bear
Nails
Hammer
Wood
Saw
Some String
A big Sheet.
One Bear bicycle
two extra bicycle chains
A Propeller
and one Small Armchair
Just big enough to fit Joe.

"LET'S DO IT!" said Joe.

Chapter 2
TAKE OFF!

They went to the top of Bear Hill.

First Harriet drew a picture of the Bear Pedal Plane.

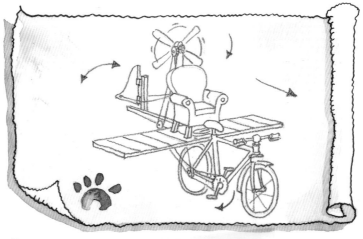

Then they made a frame for the plane,
and two wings.

Bang! Bang! Bang!

"Tie the frame onto my bear bicycle,"
Harriet said.

Joe tied the frame to the bicycle.

He ran the first chain down to the pedals.

Harriet put the second chain on the propeller.

"What's the armchair for?" Joe wanted to know.

"You sit there and steer," Harriet said.

She tied the bear armchair onto the frame.

The big sheet was tucked underneath, in case they might need it.

"My pedaling turns the propeller.
That's what makes the plane fly,"
explained Harriet Bear. "That's why this
is called a Bear Pedal Plane."

The bears put on their crash helmets.
They climbed into the Bear Pedal Plane.

"Now we pedal down the hill and fly off the big bump at the bottom," said Harriet.

"Right!" said Joe, getting excited.

"Hold on tight!" said Harriet, as they pedaled downhill.

"We're taking off, Joe!" yelled Harriet, as they came to the bump.

"Five, four, three, two, one, zero ... BLAST OFF!" shouted Joe.

"We're in the air!" called Harriet, as they soared off the bump.

"Wheeee!" yelled Joe.

Harriet pedaled as fast as she could, to keep the plane up in the air.

They flew high in the sky, over the trees in Bear Wood.

"Look at me flying!" cheered Joe.

But …

"This is really hard work," grunted Harriet, pedalling hard.

Then …

"Oh dear," puffed Harriet.

"We've stopped flying!" cried Joe, looking down at the ground.

"I'm a busted bear!" gasped Harriet.
"I'm so out of breath I can't pedal!"

"We're going to crash land on the trees in Bear Wood," yelled Joe.

The plane headed straight for the ground.

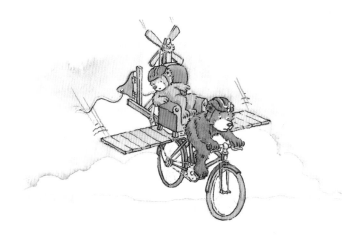

Chapter *3*

Harriet Has a Plan!

"Save me, Harriet!" wailed Joe.

"I'm thinking as fast as I can," said Harriet.

"Then think faster," said Joe.

"I've got it!" said Harriet. "Use the big sheet I put under your chair. It will be our bear parachute."

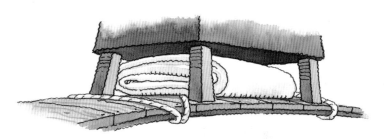

"I *knew* you'd have a Plan!" gasped Joe.
And that's what they did.

It was the best two-bear parachute ever,
and it was invented by Harriet.

The bears landed in Mother Bear's
cabbage patch.

"What have you been doing?" asked
Mother Bear.

"Joe wanted to fly, so we flew," said
Harriet.

"Don't be silly," said Mother Bear.
"Bears can't fly."

"WE JUST DID!" said Joe.

Joe Bear Goes Exploring

Chapter *1*

Joe Bear Reads a Book

One day, Joe Bear got a book from the library. The book was about bear explorers.

Joe Bear read it all at one time before he had his snack.

He read it again after his snack.

Then he went looking for Harriet Bear.

"We're having a Bear Expedition," he
told Harriet Bear. "We're going where no
bear has been before.

"I will be leader. I have to go first
because I thought of it. I've read all about
it in my library book."

They went to a part of Bear Wood
where they'd not been before.

The trees there were tall and dark.
They blotted out most of the moonlight.
"Are you there, Harriet Bear?" asked
Joe Bear, turning around.

"I'm right behind you,"
said Harriet Bear.

The further they went into Bear Wood the darker it was. Brambles spread all over the path.

They had to push their way through.

"Just follow me," said Joe Bear. "I am your leader."

"Is that so?" said Harriet Bear.

"Yes, it is," said Joe Bear, proudly.

Harriet Bear looked around her.
She'd never been that way before.
"Which way do we go?" she asked.

"Don't bother me now," said Joe Bear.
He sounded very important. "I have to be
sure that we're on the right path."

They walked a bit more.

"Where are we now?" asked Harriet
Bear. "We have to be home before
bedtime, Joe Bear."

"Ha-ho-ha-hum," said Joe Bear, pretending that he hadn't heard her.

They came to a place where two paths crossed.

Joe Bear stopped and looked around. He didn't know which way to go.

"Are we lost, Joe Bear?" said Harriet Bear.

And they were.

Chapter 2

Joe Bear Climbs a Tree

"We might need one of your Bear Plans to get us safe home, Harriet Bear," said Joe Bear.

They both stood very still.

Harriet worked on her Plan.

"Can you find a big tree for me?" asked Harriet Bear.

"There's one over there," said Joe Bear.

"Good job, Joe Bear," said Harriet Bear.

"What do I do with the tree?" asked Joe Bear.

"Can you climb it?" asked Harriet Bear.

"I'm a brown bear," said Joe Bear. "I'm the best climber there is."

He climbed to the top of the tree and looked down below.

"Can you see the moon from up there?" called Harriet Bear.

"The moon's over there,"
said Joe Bear. He pointed.

"Your house is at the end
of the wood where the moon
rises," said Harriet Bear.
"The moon-path will take us
straight home."

Joe Bear climbed down from the tree.

"This way!" he shouted. "Just follow me, Harriet Bear."

Harriet Bear followed Joe Bear through the trees.

"Hurry up, Harriet Bear," said Joe Bear. "We have to get home before bedtime."

"Almost home now!" called Joe Bear.

When they got to Bear Cottage,
Mother Bear was waiting.

"Where have you been?" asked Mother
Bear.

"We've been where no bear has been
before," said Harriet Bear.

"I took care of Harriet Bear," said Joe
Bear.

"That's just what you did," said Harriet
Bear. "You brought us safely back home."

About the author

The "Exploring" story came first.

I'd listened to a slightly older child letting a smaller child seem to win a word game, and I'd watched the moon hang over the trees in the woods near my house.

Suppose two little bears were out in the woods, and the smaller bear believed he was lost ... how could the bigger bear help him solve his problem?

Looking and listening ... that's how I find stories.